DARK AURORA

ALEXANDER SEMENYUK

This is a work of fiction. Names, characters, places, and incidents are products of the author's imagination or are used fictitiously and are not to be construed as real. Any resemblance to actual events, locations, organizations, or persons, living or dead, is entirely coincidental.

World Castle Publishing, LLC
Pensacola, Florida
Copyright © 2025 Alexander Semenyuk
Paperback ISBN: 9798891263543
eBook ISBN: 9798891263550
First Edition World Castle Publishing, LLC, March 28, 2025
http://www.worldcastlepublishing.com

Cover: Cover Designs by Karen

Editor: Karen Fuller

Dedicated to my son, Alexander George Semenyuk,
who came up with the title "Dark Aurora"
for me. I love you, Son, always.

CHAPTER ONE
THE MISSION

Kjell

Spinning, circling, the long, powerful mechanical extensions never seemed to stop moving. I don't know what they called those. I am just a soldier. And there isn't much for me to do among these scientists.

Thanks to these rotating technologies, somehow, the scientists have been able to provide us with artificial gravity on this space station— rather, a large space shuttle.

Sure, I'm thankful to them. As I got off my bed and felt my feet touch the cold floor, I was even more thankful. With a glass of sparkling water, I went to the window and watched Earth get smaller and smaller. *Goodbye, see you later, alligator. Or not. Who cares, honestly*, I thought. *It's a good, high-paying job.* I smiled as I sipped my drink, remembering the recruiting day.

It was a muggy, rainy evening. People had lined up in front of a large grey door. These were desperate times. Most jobs were done by robots, yet this rare opportunity was for a human. I wore my old tight blue jacket and stained jeans. I wasn't even sure why I was attempting this. Everyone else in line was more qualified than I. Broke ex-astronauts, high-level soldiers, secret police members, celebrity bodyguards—they'd all lost jobs to robots as well.

As I had. A regular ex-soldier, replaced by the lowest level robot combat unit. They said it was an "honorable discharge." Hilarious.

As I stood there, a dangerous situation quickly unfolded before my eyes. A tiny green toy plane flew into the center of the road, followed by a small blond boy in a blue jacket. It all happened quickly. Without even thinking, I ran into the road, snatched up the kid, and managed to get the boy and myself out of the way just barely in time. Most of those in line gasped in astonishment. The car just kept on going.

The boy was sobbing next to me, sitting on the hard asphalt. A skinny man with a long, thin nose, wearing a fancy red suit, ran towards us. "Lucas! Lucas, my boy!" He picked up the child, letting out a ragged sigh. The man held the boy tightly, kissing him on the head. Then he put Lucas down and placed a hand on my shoulder. Eyes wet, he said, "Please, write down your number for me. I will not forget this. Thank you."

I waved my hand dismissively and slowly got up. "Don't worry about it. The main thing is that the kid is okay. You take care." I smiled at Lucas and walked back to my spot in line. A couple of men had saved it for me. It was rare to see that kind of decency these days.

With little hope, I stood in that line for another hour. Finally, my turn came up. Two men in black suits led me into a hallway. We turned and came to a tall silver door which was guarded by a humanoid robot that looked like a woman. You could always tell by their eyes and shoulder and movement if you had the eye for it. These days the companies made them look so real. The robot introduced itself as "Lin," so I guess I had to refer to it as a she now. Lin scanned me, and I was allowed into the room.

I was astonished to see the very same skinny man with the thin nose, wearing his fancy red suit, sitting at the center of the table, with a petite young woman in a white suit on his left and a stern man in a military uniform on his right. I could see the skinny man's eyes sparkle as he saw me. He was almost smiling.

The stern military guy spoke first. "Kjell Johansson." He looked over to the woman at his far left. "Looks like your countryman, eh, Astrid."

She smiled and made no comment.

"So, Kjell." He continued looking at me. "What makes you think, with this resume, that you could be a good fit for this mission?"

I tried not to shrug. "I don't have ambitions. I just do my job."

The military man seemed to be stunned at my answer for a moment. The young woman looked like she was ready for the next candidate. The military man smiled and shook his head, but as he was about to speak, he was interrupted by the man in the middle.

"You're hired, Kjell. Training begins today."

The woman and military officer opened their mouths to protest, but the skinny man brought his finger to his thin nose in a "shush" motion.

I realized this was Stilton, the owner of the mission, the first trillionaire.

He spoke. "It is final. Tell everyone else that they can come back tomorrow for the second spaceship position."

And that's how I got here. Sometimes, things in life were just as simple as the water glass in my hand.

Doing something for a person that connected with their soul could make all the difference in the world. In my case, it was saving that little boy. And now I was on a spaceship headed for Mars with that very same young woman, Astrid, who was a top scientist and astronaut and certainly wasn't fond of me.

There were two robots with us. One with a male name and one female. I placed the empty glass on the table and walked away from the window. I kept thinking of Astrid. Perhaps it was the feeling of the taboo, something forbidden, that sparked so much interest, but honestly, it was most likely just the idea of annoying her and having fun at it while killing time. I was professional, and I studied the basics, but I loved to pretend I didn't get some simple things just to exasperate her. Her attitude showed she wasn't sure if I was dumb or just pretending, but either way, it irritated her greatly.

I put on my tight black outfit and went out into the hallway. At the far end I could see robot Tugworth doing something with the wires in the wall. The two robots always knew where we were but only acknowledged us when something needed to be done. I walked past Tugworth and he did not make any indication that he noticed, but I knew he did. Creepy.

The room I entered next was the botanic preservation room with many plants in glass domes, carefully attended by Astrid and another creepy helper, Bella the robot. Astrid was there now, looking at some cut-open stem on the table. Her hair looked shorter than usual; she must have cut it. Through the further glass door, I could see Bella, redheaded with pale skin, gently taking care of some green vines. Couldn't I use these robots for a massage? Heh. I approached Astrid, smirking.

"Good morning. Are you using the shower soon? I was thinking of going there."

She gave me a quick, annoyed glance and shook her head. It was Tuesday, and we were only allowed to use the shower room on Wednesdays; we both knew that. So, she remained quiet. No sense of humor. I leaned forward a bit, smiling.

"A coffee, perhaps?"

Astrid put down her tools. "We aren't allowed a coffee in here, Kjell."

"Oh yes, my mistake. Well, I'll go have one. Join me if you'd like."

Obviously, she wouldn't like, as she seemed relieved that I was leaving. Ah, Astrid. I imagined her to be that annoying, obnoxious nerd in school who everyone hated, but then when I found out that she'd been homeschooled, it hit me. Of course. To reach such heights a person couldn't go through basic or normal methods. As much as I liked to irritate her, I also understood who was. The top astro-scientist in the nation.

Not a so-called jack of all trades, but a queen of all trades. That's why they had her going to Mars to set it all up.

The previous mission, for whatever reason, had failed. They'd set up the colony buildings and the base but then lost contact and were never heard from again. Now, with a new, much bigger company, a top scientist, and a second ship full of military experts who also happened to be brilliant in other fields and new-generation robots, it all seemed too good to fail. Of course, there was me too, the lucky one.

I came to the circular kitchen and chose my coffee. It was amazing how comfortable and luxurious this flight was, at least for me, simply acting as a helper and guard. I'd imagine that I was going to do much more work upon our arrival on Mars, but that was still half a year away.

Oh yes…there was also the training. I stretched for thirty minutes every time I woke up and did the same before I went to sleep. I had to do three hours of physical training a day, which included cardio, resistance bands, reflexes, and lifting. Then, I had to do one hour a day of so-called logical training. Keeping my mind sharp. However, to me that was an easy price to pay for that salary. Speaking of which, it was time to begin my training.

CHAPTER ONE
PART TWO

Astrid

It was a long and tedious day, as usual. When I finally got to sit down, my mind was racing. It seemed that there wasn't a moment during this mission that I could relax.

It started long before we even left Earth. Being a perfectionist wasn't easy, and it was a lot harder knowing that Stilton had hired Kjell based on that man saving his young son and nothing else. He'd made an emotional hire for a very unique and sensitive position. Although, now on board, I had to say that besides being very annoying, Kjell actually performed all of his basic duties and stayed within all the rules, regulations, and protocols. Though he was competent, every member of the other ship's crew was 100 times more qualified.

Ahhh…I drank half of the cool water I had in the plain white mug and looked closer at the plant analysis from today. I was pleased with how they were handling the transition, but it seemed that the artificial light adjustment wasn't matching the natural process. That is the Martian process, as that's what we had to imitate here. The plan was to create a botanic center on Mars' surface. A dome with special glass was already there, waiting for it. The plants would be constantly regulated with the mist mixtures I had to create to achieve the right balance. Then, there was the growing of the seeds, fruits, and vegetables.

I could only deeply sigh and hold my head. I knew that the personnel on the second ship would support me upon arrival, but right now, I was so overwhelmed. I was even tempted to talk back to that imbecile, Kjell, just to get my mind off all the worrisome tasks for a bit.

CHAPTER TWO
THE SECOND SHIP

The light in the long metallic hallway flickered a bit. There was something, or someone, at the very end in the shadows. A little spark in the dark, then a cigarette dropped to the floor like a dead fly, and a merciless black boot crushed it.

He wasn't supposed to smoke, but addictions were not easy to overcome. A tall, very fit man stepped into the flickering light. His face was the color of a bone, the most pale skin someone could ever have. The thin face had a hawkish nose and high cheekbones. His eyes sat deep and had great focus. He wore all black.

Dalton smoked, but in his opinion, it was a blessing that he hadn't started using other drugs after the Great War. He was a top sniper, the very top one. There was no glory in it for him, as the faces of those he had killed haunted him, not only showing up in his nightmares but also in everyday shadows and mirrors.

Dalton was about to enter his room when he felt a firm hand on his shoulder. He knew who it was and why. His head hanging slightly, he turned, still looking defiant. The man who stood in front of him was the mission leader, Jack. He had also been Dalton's commander during the war. Jack's face was stern, and his blue eyes pierced through Dalton's.

"How many times will we have to go over this, Dalton?"

"I'm sorry, Commander." Dalton

looked at the floor.

Jack's intense blue eyes narrowed. "Every time you say sorry, where are you hiding them? If you don't put the remaining ones in my hands right now, I am suspending your pay for the mission."

Dalton's eyes widened as he was about to protest, but then he remembered whom he was talking to. Jack never threatened; he made promises and statements. If Dalton wasn't going to give, he'd be suspended. Dalton went into the room, opened a secret compartment below his bed, and carried out twenty remaining cigarettes. Jack took one of them into his left hand and, with his right, squeezed and ruined the other 19. He then gave Dalton the one.

"You can hide that one, and when we get to Mars, you can celebrate. But that's it."

Dalton smiled. Jack was stern, but he also always found ways to keep his soldiers somewhat pleased.

"Thank you, commander, I'll sleep now. My shift is in three hours."

"Good." Jack marched down the hallway as Dalton closed the door.

Up ahead was the main control room, and that's where Jack was headed. He'd been summoned by the captain and pilot of their spaceship, Stanislas.

Doors slid open, and Jack came into quite a tense scene. The whole crew, with shaved heads, was silent. Frank, a large, muscular man, was standing with his arms crossed, leaning against the wall, staring at the large screen hanging in the center of the room. Gary, the British scientist with a military background, stood leaning over a metal table with his hands firmly pressed against the surface. He was staring at the same screen. Stanislas sat in his chair with his legs crossed, also staring at the screen. The only one not doing so was the robot, Juniper, a male personality model with short black hair. He was doing something on the computer.

Jack walked up to Stanislas and put his hand on the chair. "What is this?" On the screen, he could see a large black spaceship. "Why are you watching a movie?"

Stanislas slowly turned his head toward Jack and made an unpleasant grimace. "Seriously, Jack? Do you know what this ship is?"

Jack looked back at the screen. Suddenly, his eyes got big, and his jaw slightly dropped. He quickly rushed to the coordinates panel. After checking, he turned to Stanislas, looking shocked. "How is this possible? It's almost upon us. But…but…it was believed to have been lost on Mars!"

Stanislaus rubbed his hand over his forehead. "Someone…or something… must have triggered the return sequence. We have to get on board and reprogram it. I already contacted the mission center. They are very excited." He shook his head. "I'm rather shocked. I don't have a good feeling about this."

Jack stared at the screen, incredulous. "The Dark Aurora…the crew that disappeared on Mars, right next to us. This is…bizarre."

"I have tried to make contact with the ship multiple times. There has been no reply; however, our scans indicate life forms." Stanislaus looked grim.

"Surviving crew members?"

"Why don't they reply then?"

Jack wracked his brain. "Perhaps they are unable? Trapped, injured?"

Stanislas shook his head. "If they were trapped or injured for so long, they'd also be dead. No..this is something else. Do you remember the reports? The cave next to which they set up the colony domes?"

"They reported that they saw 'something' before they went silent," Jack replied.

"Exactly." Stanislas pointed towards the screen. "That 'something' is on that ship, and the command center wants us to see what it is. Not a good plan."

"It's not supposed to be fun, Stan. We are being paid a lot for this mission. If we must take care of it, we will. Dark Aurora cost a fortune. I imagine bringing it back will get us a handsome bonus."

Stanislaus blew out his breath in frustration. "They never revealed all the documents and reports to us, Jack. There is a reason for that, don't you think?"

"What are you saying?"

"I'm saying that there is something on that ship that is not so pleasant, and they know more about it than we do."

"Don't you think they'd tell us since they want their ship back?" Jack countered.

"Not everything is a secret or a cover-up, my friend."

Jack turned to Gary and Frank. "Men, suit up and get Dalton. We will all go on board the Dark Aurora. Juniper will stay here with our ship, and once we secure Dark Aurora, Juniper will come on board and fly it back to Earth, and we will continue with our mission."

Stanislas was shaking his head. He was not as obedient a soldier as Jack was. It was never simple with him. He was a rebel, and the only reason he had been chosen for this mission was that he was a genius at his craft. The best pilot money could buy.

Jack smiled at Stanislas' frustration. "You're welcome to stay with the robot, Stan. Don't get a boo-boo."

In that moment, Stanislas' eyes became filled with fire. "I'm not a coward. Simply not a grunt who takes any orders. I'll go, don't you fret."

Jack maintained his smile. It was

hard to get under his skin, a skin thicker than a rhino's. A soldier with twenty years of experience in the most terrible spots. "Good, Stan, because we might need your skills in there."

"Haven't you watched any movies about this, man?" retorted Stan.

"Nope. I was too busy with real life. Suit up, Stan. I see Juniper is ahead of us."

They both looked at the screen. It indicated that their ship would be docking to Dark Aurora in one hour.

CHAPTER THREE
STORY TIME

Kjell

I could never get used to this in a good way. Lying in my soft bed, enjoying the calm instrumental music that helped wake me. Watching actual space from the ship's window. Such a privilege, all because of one moment. One split-second decision.

Life is a mystery.

And speaking of which, I was still a bit shaken up from the strange nightmare I'd just had. There was a tunnel or some kind of a dark place. Yes, perhaps a long, dark one because I did not remember seeing an end to it. There were indescribable creatures, their dark bodies wiry and strangely shaped. Their tiny red eyes moved around their bodies as they crawled upon the walls of that strange place. And they spoke to me, but not in any language. They spoke to my psyche, through feelings, straight into the depths of my mind.

When I woke up to the calm music, I wasn't sure if it was fear I was feeling or a studious moment. I felt as if I had learned something but couldn't quite figure out what. So strange. A mystery, yes.

I got up and got dressed. The day before, Astrid had actually spoken to me without getting too agitated, or at least I thought so. I made a big effort to avoid making the silly jokes she seemed to hate, so I think that helped, too. She said today we'd play cards, some game she knew as a kid.

Man...she probably didn't get to enjoy life much. I wondered how early she'd lost that inner child feeling. Sooner than I had, for sure, but now mine was far gone as well. Now, I was just a burnt-out soldier, happy to get a break.

With these thoughts, I walked out into the hallway and went to look for her. To my surprise, I found her sitting in the kitchen, not working. There was some freshly brewed coffee in a black mug on the table in front of her. She was shuffling some cards. When she noticed me, she slightly nodded and pointed at the cards. "Up for a few rounds?"

"As long as I get some coffee, too!"

"I'll be right here."

I walked to the machine behind her and chose the ground coffee I wanted. Strong, very strong. I sat across from her with my white mug and took the first sip. Nothing beat that first sip. Ahh.

"Astrid, you have any strange dreams lately?"

"No, why? Are you having some?"

"Yeah…"

She looked at me closely. "Sometimes this happens in space. You read the notebook, right?"

I chuckled. "Eh…hehe."

She gave me a look of disapproval. "Well, what kind of dreams?"

"They start with me floating in space but then end up in a strange tunnel with some sort of creatures."

"Have you been listening to the approved brain wave recordings?"

"Oh no," I shrugged.

She fixed me with a withering look. "Kjell, those help regulate the psyche, helping you to sleep better." Astrid shook her head.

Suddenly, a red light lit up above us, and there was a long beep. Astrid stood up swiftly, a worried look on her face. I knew this was another one of those things I should have read about in the instructions.

CHAPTER THREE
PART TWO

Astrid

After the emergency transmission alarm, the two robots, Tugworth and Bella, were standing in the doorway looking like an odd couple, waiting for my command. Kjell was still sitting with his coffee... God, he must have not read about this either..."Kjell, let's go. It's an emergency message from the command center back on Earth."

He put down his coffee and followed me into the hallway, as did the robots. It was strange having all three behind me and being the leader of the pack. I had always viewed myself as someone who just did her work in the background. This leadership role was rather nerve-wracking.

Upon entering the bridge, we all focused on the communication screen. A robotic face appeared and began delivering the message: "This is the message to Mission Ship One. The Second Ship is currently stopped because of another engagement. It appears that they found the lost ship, Dark Aurora. They are about to go aboard. You are to proceed with your course and the mission to Mars. The second team will join you upon directing Dark Aurora back to Earth. End of message."

For a moment, I was taken aback by the shock. My mentor, Doctor Liardes, was presumed to have died after landing on Mars in that ship, Dark Aurora.

I saw Kjell looking at me with a concerned face. "What is this Dark Aurora, Astrid? I've only vaguely heard of this, the original mission that established those Mars domes we are supposed to reactivate, right?"

I slowly sat up straight. This deserved a proper answer. "Listen, Kjell, I will tell you all that I know about the Dark Aurora mission.

"You might have heard and watched a lot from the mainstream news, but the truth is very different. Fifteen years ago, the spaceship Dark Aurora was complete and ready to launch. The mission leader was none other than the mentor I had in my youth, the world-renowned Doctor Liardes, accompanied by the great astrophysicist Professor

Harvik, six skilled astronauts, and two robots. The mission, as you know, was to finally establish the first real Mars colony."

I took a breath and went on. "Dark Aurora was an incredibly large spaceship. The Titanic of Space and the first of its kind. Inside, it was carrying the domes, gardens, rovers—everything needed to establish the colony. Dark Aurora had a similar gravity system to the one we are using now, as well.

"Everything was going smoothly. The crew was able to land on Mars. Yet, there was just one troubling sign. Doctor Liardes reported that Harvik was having breakdowns and hallucinations. At the time, this was considered a normal thing during long space travel."

Kjell was staring at me, eyes wide.

I stood up and walked around as I continued, "The colony was established and the domes were all connected by thick glass hallways. The technology of this glass also blocked most of the radiation and there were filters installed for cleaning the air and producing enough from the plants being grown in the largest dome, the garden.

"It was when the crew found a cave in the mountain next to the colony that things began to go wrong. Harvik would not stop venturing into this cave, and eventually, he took two other crew members with him. However, only he emerged from there. According to Liardes, Harvik was frantic, speaking of creatures that had no proper shapes. He spoke of the need to share their wisdom." I sat down once again.

The look on Kjell's face was incredulous. "The crew isolated Harvik, but he managed to leave the cell. The last transmission we got was from Liardes, saying that he and the few remaining members were getting on board the Dark Aurora to escape Harvik. It seems that Harvik managed to reprogram the two robots to attack the crew. In the very last part of the message Liardes said that he was seeing 'something' moving towards the ship.

"This is when we lost all contact with Dark Aurora as it left Mars. No life was detected in the colony after that. It took a long time to plan out and gather for this next mission."

Kjell looked stunned at the story. He slowly shook his head. "Wow. So... Harvik went insane, used robots to kill the crew, and the ship has been floating in space until now? And what was this 'something?'"

I shrugged. "That's unknown, but it could have just been hallucinations as well. This is why our protocols, diet, training, and new brain wave devices are all so crucial. The mental health of the crew is key to this mission's success."

"Let's hope they deal with it fast so there isn't a big delay. I'd imagine setting everything up on our own would be rough."

I squared my shoulders and narrowed my eyes. "I'm trained for it."

CHAPTER FOUR
DARK AURORA

They were known as Team Sphere Five. Of course Jack and the others did not refer to themselves as that.

Once the two ships established full connection, the team of five elite men put on their black suits with rather slim-looking atmosphere helmets and walked into the connector tunnel. They stood before the round metal exterior door of Dark Aurora. All five could feel the tension in the air. Each one of the men had a great intuition for danger, and right now, all five were feeling this sense to the maximum.

"Well, Stanislas, crack open the

code to the door, will you? Haven't got all day," said Jack, trying to instill confidence and calmness into the team.

Stanislas came up to a panel and plugged in a device. Various numbers appeared on the screen. The team patiently waited. Then a click came, and ominously, the heavy round door slowly slid open.

First, there was nothing but darkness within the spaceship. Then there was a small flash of light, a broken panel on the wall.

Jack stepped in first with Dalton, the thin-faced, pale sniper right behind him. Once the whole team was inside, they turned on the small flashlights on top of their helmets, and Jack gestured at the door. "Close it."

Big Frank looked worried for

a moment, but Stanislas did not countermand the order. The door slid closed again. "If there is something strange here, we don't want it onboard our ship also," explained Jack and motioned for them to move.

Dark Aurora was the size of a small town. It was the largest spaceship ever created. As the team went further into the first dark hallway, a strange sound filled the air. It was almost like one prolonged hissing of a snake accompanied by a constant low vibration.

"What the hell is this, mate…?" the Brit, Gary, shook his head. "Definitely not normal, I tell ya. Not my type of party."

Jack forged ahead. "Just keep moving, slow, stay alert. Stanislas, you know the layout the best, which way to the command center?"

"Well, from this entrance, we must make it to the first-floor information room, go up the stairs, and take the elevator to the fourth, top floor. From there, across the bridge will be the center, apparently a square room overlooking much of the ship."

"Like a robot, well done, my friend. So, straight ahead until we reach a big room on this floor, yes?"

"Correct, Jack."

A beastly scream came from the distant darkness.

Jack took a knee and pulled out his laser pistol. Dalton leaned against the wall and aimed his rifle. The other three situated themselves behind Jack with their automatic Taurus 77 machine guns.

Jack could hear their breathing. The strange hissing continued all around him. Then another scream came, this time much closer.

"Get ready!"

Out of the darkness a strange creature came running. It almost had no proper shape to describe. Its three long arms had sharp needle-like claws, and its dark head was almost liquid-looking, changing shapes as it ran upon four wiry legs.

They all began to fire. Laser, bullets, an explosive sniper round to the head. The monster got a taste of it all. Its body was ripped to shreds as severed arms and legs convulsed on the floor.

"What is that, Jack?" asked Frank in a deep, shaky voice.

"Get to the command center, and we might find out what happened here. Move."

The team sped up the pace, moving past pieces of the monster. Up ahead, they could see a large opening. The central information room, or more of a gathering hall.

As they exited the corridor, they were met with hundreds of horrific screams, some the same as the previous one, some different. The team moved their heads around using their flashlights and quickly realized that even stranger monsters were coming down the walls from all sides.

"Back, fall back!" Jack yelled.

They frantically ran back towards the doorway, but the creatures were gaining fast, screaming, clawing, hissing right behind them.

Stanislas yelled out, "No time, Jack, run past the door. We have to get to the botanic section and seal ourselves there. It's on the other corridor!"

Just then, some of the creatures reached them. Frank began to shoot. "Go, go, go! I've got this!"

Jack hesitated for a moment, but he knew better; there was no way they'd survive if they stayed to help Frank, and his sacrifice would be wasted. "Hurry, men, hurry!"

As they sprinted after Jack, a larger creature emerged from the darkness and pierced Frank with its long, thin arm. It lifted him up and ran a long tentacle into him. He screamed out in horrific pain as other creatures fed on him.

Meanwhile, the team reached the heavy door of the botanic section. Stanislas worked fast to unlock it, and they immediately sealed it.

Gary and Stanislas both sat against the wall, breathing heavily, Jack stood gathering his thoughts as quickly as he could, and Dalton was looking around. To his shock, some of the large plants with vines were still alive; there were bushes and trees as well.

"How…what…" he shook his head. "Hasn't this ship been lost for 14 years now?"

"Yeah…and those…monsters, do they feed on each other? Did they keep the crew somewhere?" Dalton shook his head. However, their break was about to come to an end, as they heard a dragging sound and then a low growl coming from behind some bushes.

Stanislas and Gary rose to their feet and aimed the weapons.

There emerged a sort of half-man.

His face had a dark growth that looked like a fungus, his eyes were bloodshot red, he was dragging his own giant overgrown arm, and there was a second mouth in the middle of his chest.

Gary shook his head vigorously. "Here comes the damn gardener!"

Jack's eyes expanded as he recognized who it was. "It's professor Harvik," he said, his voice hushed with shock.

"Or at least what's left of his body, eh?" said Dalton and pulled the trigger. The bullet hit Harvik directly in the head, blowing half of it away. Harvik fell on his knees, but then the particles of the head began to come back and regrow almost immediately.

Jack motioned towards the upper floor. "Move now! Run up!"

They turned away from the horrific sight and ran past a tall tree with many vines and into a small office with glass windows. They bolted the door and watched as Harvik slowly made his way up the steps, dragging his large arm.

"What's worse, a slow, indestructible one, or a thousand fast but killable?"

"Shut up, Gary." Stanislas plugged his small device into a panel and a map appeared on a small screen.

"There, we have to get to the other side of this floor, where there's an elevator. We take it up to the fourth and…"

The glass shattered as Harvik smashed the windows with one swing of his deformed arm. Dalton shot him twice in the head, and the team jumped through the broken glass and ran toward the other side of the floor.

As they ran, Jack noticed the bottom door leading to the hallway was almost broken, with thousands of screams coming from behind it. "Hurry! They are breaking through!"

Adrenaline was pushing the team to their limits as they rushed to the elevator, and Stanislas activated it. The monsters broke through into the botanical garden, but the elevator doors closed only seconds before they reached it.

There was no time to rest. The second elevator stopped on the fourth floor, and everyone ran after Stanislas as he led the way toward the command center. The screams, roars, and hissing around them intensified.

They finally had the bridge in their sights, but a swarm of creatures crawled out right in front of it, looking like a bunch of spiders. A larger one lifted itself up onto the bridge. It was dark and deformed, with six long arms, three heads, and two legs. It slowly looked at them with its red eyes that seemed to be moving side to side, almost floating in the darkness of its face.

"Here!"

They entered a small square interior room and slammed the metal door, which had a tiny glass window at the top.

The room was empty, and both Gary and Stanislas sat against the door. Dalton leaned over and put his hands on the wall, setting his rifle aside. Jack backed away to the opposite wall and leaned on it. They all turned off their helmet lights and Jack pointed out a single small bright cube on the floor.

"What now, mate? All finished, aren't we?" asked Gary, looking at Jack.

Jack shook his head. "Never finished until it's actually finished."

"So, what do we do?" asked Stanislas.

"Command room. Unbreakable glass, correct?"

"Yes."

Jack thought a moment. "If the computers are activated, can we communicate with Earth?"

"Yes, I think so," replied Stanislas. "By the way, we can't get a signal to send a message to Juniper on our devices."

"We noticed."

"So, how do we get into that center

then?" Dalton finally straightened up and joined the conversation.

Jack's mouth was set in a thin line. "We keep watching that small window. Whenever their numbers go down, we rush for it."

"Some, if not all of us, will die." Gary shook his head.

"Does everyone know how to get the transmissions going to Earth?"

Stanislas and Dalton nodded, but Gary shook his head. "Damn, mate, I guess that means I'm most expendable."

"No one is. Not among us. We will all go out there together. Keep watching that window. We take shifts watching it," Jack said, determinedly.

"What if it never clears?" asked Dalton.

"Then we will go when we have no

more supplies."

"Mate, we only have a pouch each, so that won't be long at all," Gary looked down into his.

"Up to two days."

"Well, I best confess my sins to you guys now. No priest is available. Unless Professor Harvik can land a big hand," Gary laughed.

"Shit man! How can you joke now!" yelled Stanislas.

"You must be forgetting our good old Gary. Even under the metro bombing at the battle of D.C., this guy was telling jokes," said Dalton, dryly.

Stanislas shook his head and made no further comment.

Jack came up to Gary. "Sure, buddy, what's on your mind?" Gary's face changed and became serious, and he stood up and shook Jack's hand. "You always understand me, mate. Just a few things I want you to know and to tell a few people for me if I die and you live. Is that all right?"

"Of course, Gary, go on."

"To my mom, tell her that it was I who broke her blue vase, not that silly dog, Jonny. That pup was the best."

Jack smiled at put his hand on Gary's shoulder.

"And to my brother. Tell him that I lied about letting him beat me in boxing. He really did. And tell both that I love them. All right?"

"Yes, Gary, but you'll say it yourself, friend. How is it out there, Dalton?"

Dalton turned away from the small window to address Jack. "Still swarming. I saw a few other huge ones, but it's dark, and hard to see. Well, honestly, just those broken lights near the bridge help a bit."

"Keep watching."

"How I wish for Barry's Irish tea right about now, dear Lord, that taste improves any atmosphere," Gary said, wistfully.

Stanislas grimly looked at Gary. In a way, he was jealous, wondering how someone could face horror, pain, and death in such a manner. Stanislas was shaking in fear. The terror was overtaking him; there were voices inside his head telling him to open the door and run.

Dalton noticed Stanislas grimacing on the floor and shaking his head. "You okay there, our man map? Don't break on us now. We need you."

"Yes, yes, let me be on watch now."

"Sure thing, buddy, go on then."

Stanislas pressed his face against the glass. Far away in the darkness, he saw two narrow, dark red eyes. They belonged to a slim figure standing among the swarm and it was speaking directly into his mind, whispering to him, telling him to run out and enjoy the power, to join the hive.

"Yes! Yes!" frantically yelled Stanislas, and opened the door, running out.

"Go now, to the bridge!" yelled Jack.

They ran out and opened fire, clearing the way onto the bridge. But Stanislas ran away from the bridge and towards the dark figure. He was seized by the creatures and pinned down to the floor. They were coming nonstop. One of them managed to slice Gary's chest open, and he fell to the floor right in front of the bridge, still blasting away, before the creatures swarmed over him. A tiny one jumped upon Jack's shoulder and bit him. Dalton blasted it away but was stabbed through his stomach by a long tentacle in the process. Jack pulled him away, fell into the command center, and slammed the large unbreakable glass door behind him.

He quickly examined his surroundings. The command room was clear. He opened a panel on the side wall, and dim lights came on in the room. Dalton was moaning on the floor, and Jack helped him sit up.

"There must be a medical kit here."

"Stop." Dalton put his hand on Jack's shoulder. "You know very well that would be futile. Look at the size of this wound."

Out of the inner pocket of his suit, Dalton pulled out a single cigarette and a lighter. "Thanks for leaving this one for me, Commander."

Those were his final words as he got a single puff on the cigarette before keeling over, lifeless.

Jack stood in the center of the room motionless, gathering his thoughts. His shoulder throbbed in pain from the bite. He had lost everyone. The best team. He closed his eyes in sorrow and agony.

Outside the thick glass walls and doors, he could see all the monsters. They were swarming and screaming, but the noise was muffled inside this command room. Jack approached the transmission table and activated the codes. First there was some static, then came what he had hoped for.

"Commander? Jack? Is that you? Have you guys reached the center? Is Dark Aurora secured?"

"I reached the center," Jack said, wearily. "The ship is not secured. There are hostile life forms on board."

"Where is the rest of the crew?"

A beat. "All dead."

Silence followed, and then they resumed. "How many life forms and how long can you last?"

Jack looked over at the bottom supplies cabinet. There were a bunch of liquid pouches there; he could manage on two per week. "A few months, I think. I am injured, so I'm not certain. There are possibly a thousand of the life forms on board."

"Thousand?"   The   voice   was

incredulous.

"Correct."

"Jack, we will be sending ships with the army. You hold on there."

"Sure. What about the second ship? The mission to Mars?"

"They'll continue without you."

CHAPTER FIVE
WE KEEP GOING

Kjell

When I heard that they wouldn't provide updates about the team that went into Dark Aurora, I knew it meant things had gone badly, but just how badly?

Upon receiving the news that we had to keep on going with the Mars mission on our own for sure, Astrid wasn't as tough as when she'd heard that possibility the first time. I think reality had set in. Sure, she was well trained for it all, but having multiple other experts helping versus doing it alone was very different. The systems setup, air maintenance, botanical garden, rovers going to the cave, all the equipment, journaling, data collection, and communications were all tasks that needed to be done. On top of it, we had continual training. The two robots would help, sure, and I'd do my best too, but it was gonna be tough.

I shook my head and stared into space outside the window. Somewhere out there was the second ship, attached to Dark Aurora. What had happened to them? What had gotten on board?

Hmmm. I wished I had a strong drink right about now, but none were available. I suppose it wouldn't help my IQ test that was coming up in an hour. I had to take one every week. Making sure I was staying sharp, I guess.

This stuff was funny to me. Did they think I'd decline so rapidly?

Astrid seemed to be a believer; she loved the protocols, laws, and rules. The strict boundaries seemed to make her feel safer. I understood. I'd never really had this in my life, so to change now was difficult.

I took off my clothes and went into a tall tube lined with red lights. It was time for my physical scan.

Almost all the results were fine except the brain scan. My amygdala functions lit up as irregular. A few pills dropped into a small cup. Great. More forced meds and rules. I took the pills into my mouth and swallowed with the help of some orange juice.

"Kjell, can you please report to the command center? We have to discuss a few things. There are things you have to learn to help me with before we land and it's coming up soon."

It was the speaker in my room. I clicked the purple button and replied. "I have the IQ test soon. Should I come after that?"

"Sure, I'll see you then."

CHAPTER FIVE
PART TWO

Astrid

My initial thought when Kjell asked
for a delay was to deny it, but I almost
immediately changed my mind. He was
showing himself capable of following
directions and a schedule. It was exactly
what I'd need from him once we landed
on Mars. Going through all the data
and papers now was making me feel a
bit overwhelmed. It was more work for
just one person and a few robots than
I realized. And considering that the
mission had already run into trouble
with the other ship, we could not afford

any more mistakes or problems.

As I sipped on my coffee with milk, Kjell appeared in the doorway. I motioned at the seat across from mine.

Everything Kjell did could be described as "simple" or "ordinary." His manners, walk, expression, looks. Everything. I suppose that would make him extraordinary in a funny way.

He sat down, but as his eyes moved to my coffee, I answered his next question before he asked. "Yes, you may get a coffee first."

Once that was done, he was finally ready. I laid out a few papers in front of him. "Upon arrival, I want to primarily focus on tasks that only I can do. Not you, not the robots. Bella will take care of the most basic maintenance, and Tugworth will do the electrical work and will drive the rover for you. Of course, you can learn it too. Your main task will be checking the cave and reporting on any findings there, and at the bottom of the mountain, as well. You'll also have to take the lift to where the solar panels are installed. Tugworth will get them running again with a few upgrades we are bringing, but you'll have to go up there every day to make sure all is well. Those will be an important source of energy for us."

"And the cave, every day, too?"

"Every day. Such are the instructions. This was meant for Jack, but we are taking everyone's part at this point."

"Okay, well, I'm sure I'll feel more useful." He snorted a short laugh.

"You will be very useful."

CHAPTER SIX
THE SHOWDOWN

Jack slowly got up from the floor. The muffled screams and roars had now become a background sound that he was completely used to. It had been a month.

Jack saw his reflection in the window, along with the weird, deformed face of a creature right outside of it. Jack now sported a grey beard. A young man with a grey beard...the level of stress crushed his system.

Two things he couldn't get used to were the never-ending, throbbing pain where he'd been bitten on his left shoulder and the terrifying nightmares each time he fell asleep. He repeatedly dreamed of a large black liquid diamond just floating in the air. It had black goo dripping from it. The dark, slim, red-eyed monster was always around it, whispering things Jack could never make out. Each time he woke, he felt just that bit more exhausted and on the verge of a mental breakdown.

Jack glanced at his supply box. Five more pouches left. He was close to starving himself. His arms and hands constantly shook, and his legs wobbled. He sat most of the time, just staring at the white floor. Worst of all, Stanislas had turned into a creature similar to Harvik, and he often stood by the glass door, staring inside. Jack didn't want to see that. The white floor was better.

The last transmission had promised the arrival of army support imminently. They did not lie. Seven smaller army spaceships were approaching the coordinates, almost at the destination. They were led by the famous general Barbad, a man who had a long scar across his face. It could easily have been fixed by modern medicine, but Barbad wore it with too much pride. And with pride, he also took on this extermination mission.

Little did he know what really awaited.

Six ships docked and attached to each other, with only the main one attached to the Dark Aurora. The seventh ship was attached to both the Mars mission ship and Dark Aurora. Juniper confirmed that scans of life forms had not changed, and the soldiers lined up to begin the cleansing of Dark Aurora and the rescue of the hero, Jack.

As the previous team did, they

had an expert take care of the code. The door slid open, and the chaos and madness ensued immediately, contrary to the previous team's experience. The creatures rushed into the opening, viciously attacking the soldiers. Barbad was screaming orders as they set up lines and were firing nonstop. Blood splashed all over the walls as soldiers and creatures were falling dead left and right. Immense showers of bullets and lasers covered the area of the entrance, and it took Barbad multiple shouts to get them to cease fire.

As most were breathing heavily and were either pumped or horrified, more screams came from within the ship.

"Squad One, move in. We must secure the first quadrant before more of those creatures get here. All other squads are to follow in order. Ready to fire. Flame torch squad, advance behind squad one; we will need you."

Every soldier had an ear insert and could hear Barbad's every word loud and clear. He was with Squad Three, consisting of the most elite Marines.

As the first squad got inside and set up at the bottom of the large hall, a giant, fat, dark figure slowly crawled out of the darkness at the back of the room. The creature had four heads with one big black eye in each; its lower body was like a slug's, and it dragged itself along with two gigantic claw arms.

With shaky hands, the squad aimed. As more soldiers piled in, they took aim as well.

"What the hell…" Barbad let it slip. "Fire!"

As the bullets and lasers made

contact with the monster's bizarre flesh, it let out an abnormally loud shriek, causing some soldiers to drop their weapons. From the shadows of the walls and ceiling came hundreds of dark, wiry monsters. Despite Barbad shouting commands, it mostly became disorganized, chaotic warfare.

Barbad moved into a separate corridor with his squad. The leader of the squad was named Tom, an experienced old soldier. "You know the layout map! I'm sending half of the flame torch guys with you! Go grab Jack. The rest will push on here. We gotta kill them all!" Barbad screamed.

Tom nodded, and the squad of elite Marines ran after him through the corridor. As they got farther and farther away from the fighting, the noise of it still rang all around and through the ship.

"Left!"

The team stopped for a moment. In the open room before the elevator stood Professor Harvik, who appeared to be smiling. Tom and the others opened fire.

Harvik was close enough to grab one of them and crush his body. Bullets ripped through him, and Harvik fell in pieces, but to Tom's horror, Harvik began to quickly regrow.

"Torch him!"

The flame team turned their weapons on Harvik. He let out agonizing screams and was finally turned to ashes. Relief flooded Tom and his men. He quickly barked out, "Four go up the elevator, I'll come with another four, then three torch squad follow. Eight of you stay here and wait for us to come back."

As they began the procedure the noise of the battle was becoming less intense; however, the number of screams and roars barely decreased. Tom looked into the dark corridor. "We are losing. We must hurry. Barbad was ordered to blow up this place if we didn't succeed at getting these things out."

As Tom was coming up the elevator, he heard shots. The first four men were engaged in a fight. A few of the creatures were closing in on them and he arrived just in time. He and his group held them off until the next two loads of men arrived with their flame throwers. They quickly were able to eliminate the creatures.

Across the bridge they could see the command center with its thick glass. Behind it stood Jack, waving at them and pointing up to his right, yelling something they could not hear. Jack realized his mistake and went to the room's speaker.

"Their leader is there, the thin one!"

Tom quickly looked up. On top of a large pipe stood a slim, tall, dark creature. It had two long arms and many tentacle-like thin feet. Its eyes were dark red, staring directly at Tom.

Tom felt pressure in his head. "Men, go get Jack!"

They ran toward the bridge but were cut off by a group of small monsters. They circled and took them out, taking one casualty in the process. More began to swarm as the leader started to let out a terrifying high-pitched shriek. Tom reached the door, and Jack opened it, leaning on Tom. "We will go to the opposite hallway now, towards your mission ship, Jack."

The torch team was giving them great cover as they escaped into the hallway. They reached the door, and Tom plugged in the numbers as several other men gave their lives to buy some time. They transferred onto the connector and shut the door. Frantically, they opened the mission ship's door and collapsed inside. Only seven men, along with Jack and Tom, made it.

"Tom, do you copy." It was Barbad.

"Yes. We have Jack. We are on the Mars mission ship."

"Tom, detach the ship immediately, right now. We are overwhelmed. I can't make it back. I will press the self-destruct command for our ships before they take me. This will kill the source, destroy Dark Aurora and us."

Tom's jaw dropped, and Jack stood up on wobbly legs as Juniper came to his aid.

"Detach the ship now, Juniper, leave me here. Hurry!" Jack ordered.

The robot sprinted into the commander center and initiated the process. Had he done so thirty seconds later, they would have been caught in the mighty explosion.

It was the end of Dark Aurora.

Tom stood by the window, watching in shock. Jack sat in the chair next to him.

"So many of our men. Brave men, dedicated. Just…had families. Gone like that, with a snap of your fingers. So is that demonic source…?" lamented Tom.

"Not sure, Tom. Sorry to say."

"What, no, what do you mean?"

Jack shook his head. "I've had dreams and visions. I'm sure that thing sent them to me. A cave…on Mars."

"That's where they came from, now they're dead."

"I hope you're right. To think such things existed! What if they came to Earth? They'd turn our planet into a real horror freak show. People don't know what petty things they complain about. honestly." Jack remembered his team, especially Stanislas's fate. Was his friend trapped inside the monster version of reality, or was his soul gone by then, living in a different place? He guessed someday he would find out. He hoped not too soon.

CHAPTER SEVEN
A NEW BEGINNING

Mars finally came into view in all of its glory. The so-called red planet, or the rusty metal planet more like it, Kjell thought. He stood by the main observation window next to Astrid. "How cold did you say it gets at night again, Astrid?"

She rolled her eyes. "Don't you worry. We have good heating systems, and the base is somewhat close to the equator, so we will get to the 70s in midday and use our solar panels to gather energy."

Kjell chuckled. "Heh…Well, I'm all ready for high jumps and longer days."

Astrid actually cracked a smile; the joke mixing in scientific facts was to her liking.

A large screen dominated the main wall, with red lights glowing along the sides. Astrid and Kjell joined the robots in the main command room, strapping themselves into chairs. The landing procedure was about to begin. This was always nerve-wracking as Mars posed a challenge with landings. The two robots had gone through extensive programming when it came to this procedure, as the slightest error could prove fatal. Kjell was more or less relaxed despite the odds, but Astrid was extremely tense. Kjell could see her squeezing the arms of her seat.

"Not fond of landings?!" he yelled as the ship began to shake and enter the atmosphere. Astrid ignored the comment and was nervously focused on the screen. Despite her tension, the landing was as smooth as it could be.

The ship touched down right next to the colony. Kjell rose to his feet and looked upon it in astonishment. It was far larger than he expected. The main dome was the size of a church. It was connected to five other smaller domes by glass tunnels. There was also the power station and two rovers inside a garage-type structure.

Everything was partially covered with sand. There was no connector from the ship to the disinfection center, which they had to go through in order to get into the first dome.

The robots began to unload the equipment while Kjell and Astrid put on their suits and got their personal bags.

"Quite a lot of stuff; that weak gravity will really come in handy with this load," Kjell commented.

"After we unload, we must activate the main power; it's in the second dome. After that we can rest a bit, but not long. We have to get to the basic first tasks as soon as possible, then the rest can be taken more slowly." Astrid's tone was professional and a little bossy.

Kjell grinned wryly, then asked, "When should I go into the cave?"

Astrid kept her eyes on her task as she replied, "If we clear the rovers today and they run without needing repair, you can go as soon as tomorrow."

"Lovely."

The doors opened, and they were lowered onto the Mars surface. The team took their first steps upon this foreign soil.

"Wow, my heart is beating fast. I didn't think I'd be this excited, like a kid."

Astrid looked at Kjell for a prolonged moment and smiled. She found herself thinking the very same thing. "I dreamed my whole life of something like this…"

"Well, does it match your expectations?"

"To actually be here, knowing how rare it is. I think so. We have so many people relying on us."

"Noooo pressure at all!"

"Come on."

They entered a chamber where the air pressure was changed, and they could take off their suits and hang them up. They both had key codes, and Astrid used one to open the door, which led them into the first dome.

There was old equipment, various suits hung on the walls, and a small dining area. Astrid motioned for them to move past it. "Bella will load things into this dome and clean it up. We must go to the second one with Tugworth and see if we can restore all of the power. The living quarters are…"

"In dome 3, yes, not counting the main large dome, the botanical garden."

"Correct."

CHAPTER SEVEN
PART TWO

Kjell

As we entered the second dome, I was taken aback by the strange smell and the darkness inside. This dome had a blacked-out roof. Tugworth had a large flashlight, and as he turned it on, I thought I saw something quickly move in the shadows. I glanced at the robot and Astrid. They had no reaction, and I was very tired…

The robot, Tugworth, began his work around the computers in the wall. In a few minutes, the room was lit up; however, not all the news was great.

"Only 60% of power is restored. It

is enough to run the smaller domes, but all function must be restored to begin the garden project all over again." Astrid looked over at me. "You and Tugworth have to go and see if the rovers are okay. After that, you can rest. It's going to be dark soon, and it will be too cold out. You'll go tomorrow morning to set up the panels and check the cave. I'll set everything up inside and will begin to send data and communications."

"Can I have some tea time after checking the rovers? I'm already so cold."

"After I check the living quarters I'll be on my own for the night, but you're welcome to have Bella assist you in making tea after your work."

Of course…that was fine. I nodded my head and motioned to Tugworth to hurry up. "Let's get those rovers checked, my metal buddy."

Tugworth actually looked offended and I honestly hated when these artificial imitators of life did that, but I wouldn't continue to annoy him. It? Maybe a robot could go nuts also, like having a virus, and I wouldn't want that happening here. We were in enough danger as it was.

Even with the special thermal layers inside my suit, I felt the chill outside. "Slow down your breathing, Kjell," I heard Tugworth's voice in my earpiece. Of course, our oxygen tanks, no matter how advanced, still had a limit.

"I know, I know."

"Don't get angry with me. This leads to further oxygen waste."

Shit! Can you believe this thing? I thought. *This is why they can never be like us! When in the world does anyone get less angry when you tell them to stop being angry!*

"Elevated levels…"

"Stop, Tugworth! Would you mind making no comments tonight besides anything related to the rovers?"

"Of course, Kjell. You must have a cool head to take care of the rovers well."

I shook my "hot" head, and we entered the garage, which was being cleared of sand. Most of it was sucked out by the tubes on the floor. It was fortunate that this function of the base worked with whatever level of power was restored.

I got into one of the large black rovers with Tugworth. They had dark, thermal black windows and oxygen filters inside. However, we ran a scan before lowering our tank consumption and mixing in the rover air. The scan showed the system working properly. Tugworth showed me how to turn the engine on and then slowly drove the rover out of the garage. It was surprisingly easy, or so it seemed.

When it was my turn, it took me a while. Coming back, it was even chillier than before and I was very glad once we were back inside the domes. To my delight, Tugworth went away out of sight. I remembered Astrid telling me that I wouldn't see her until the next day. With that in mind, I found Bella and asked "her" for assistance in making tea.

Despite all the time the black tea had sat on Mars, and though it had lost most of its aroma, the semi-bitter specific taste was still there. I poured it into a tall metal thermos and went into my room.

Maybe it was better described as a large closet than a room. The tiny bed took up half of it, and then there was a chair with an arm table attached. It stood next to a small circular window. I sat heavily into it, placing the thermos on the table, and with weary, tired eyes, looked out upon the cold night desert of another planet. Some thought dreams were made of this, but it was more about the nightmares…

I gazed at the dark red desert floor…dried out under a bloody sun. I stood up to look out the small window.

Despite the burning, I would not go blind—it was not as bright as Earth's sun. When I finally looked away from it, I heard a voice all around me. Like a whisper…and then I noticed him. There was a shadow which the sun couldn't put out and inside of it stood a man.

Or was it a man? A slim, tall, dark

creature with deep red eyes was speaking to me, but he had no mouth. He spoke to my mind...

A knife and a gun appeared in my hands, and all around me lay dead bodies. I panicked and screamed, and across the desert field, I saw myself, but sinister, a double...I was laughing...

I woke up and put my hand on my head, breathing heavily and feeling my heart pounding. It was still dark.

I sat up in bed and gathered my breath, controlling my heart rate. I checked the small monitor next to my bed. It indicated that there was one hour until sunlight.

There was no point in trying to sleep more, and seeing my first Mars sunrise was going to be a bonus. I picked up my wristband and called Bella, requesting strong coffee. Of course, the robot showed no surprise at the hour of the request. It was all the same to her, and in just ten minutes, I was sitting by the window and slowly sipping on the hot coffee, patiently watching the desert.

Time passed slowly and I was on my third cup. I looked down and swished around the last drops of it, and then there was light. With astonishment, I watched the sunrise over the Mars desert, feeling like a kid. They say the best time for everything is the first time. I don't agree with that for many situations, but when it comes to experiencing natural events for the first time, I imagine how few people have actually witnessed this in person. Just the Dark Aurora crew had before me. That was it, only them.

My enjoyment was broken up by

a loud message coming from a sound panel on the wall. It was Astrid.

"Kjell, please have your breakfast and get ready. We can't lose any sunlight time. Tugworth has loaded the panels on an attachment behind the rovers, and you'll need to drive both out so you can get all the panels out there. Hopefully, the lift is working."

Annoyed, I pressed the black button on the wall and replied. "It will be the longest breakfast that I'll ever have."

"I'm serious, Kjell."

With that, the contact was cut. Yet another joke of mine had annoyed her. Fine, fine. Gotta go with that robot Tugworth, such a bastard.

I ate defrosted eggs with a waffle. It was actually quite good, and I enjoyed my fourth cup of coffee.

When I walked out into the common room, Astrid was there. "You'll finish all our coffee reserves before the first week is out," she commented, sipping on her first cup.

"Look at you, cracking jokes yourself."

She almost smiled and waved when I followed Tugworth. We suited up and got into the rovers.

Tugworth took the first rover out, and then I slowly followed right behind him in the second. We both pulled panels behind, attached to four wheels.

CHAPTER EIGHT
THE DARK DIAMOND

Tugworth finished examining the lift and came back to the rover in which Kjell was saving up air.

"It's broken, Kjell. It will take an hour to fix the box, and we will be able to hoist it with the panels."

Kjell was holding a scanning tablet and pointed at a spot on it to Tugworth. "So, right around there is that cave I assume, that's just around the side of this mountain."

"Do you wish to take the rover there while I work on the lift?"

"Hmmm, I think so. This way, we can cover a few tasks at the same time."

"Is it wise to split up?"

"I don't think there is anything here that can hurt us. It all left with the Dark Aurora."

"What left?"

"Whatever evil thing there was."

"My programming suggests that they simply went mad."

"Uh yeah, programming. Well, you get to fixing and I'll get to driving. See you in one hour."

Kjell drove the rover out as Tugworth was still protesting the idea. "That robot...so annoying," he muttered.

The cave entrance was indeed nearby, and it was very easy to identify, as the previous expedition had created a large metal framed entrance for it.

Kjell stopped the rover and observed the frame. The structure looked to be made from very dark and shiny metal, something that didn't match any materials around the base, nor any that he had seen used before. A suspicious feeling crept over Kjell.

CHAPTER EIGHT
PART TWO

Kjell

This structure hadn't been built by humans, at least not the ones I knew. That was my conclusion as I observed it. Enough staring, however. I put on the helmet and made sure the air level was up to 100%. Who knew what was in there and how long I would need to take.

I went through the depressurizing chamber and then hopped out of the rover. My blaster was attached to my right hip, but for now, I was armed with only a flashlight. I left the sunny day to enter the darkness of this mysterious cave.

At first glance, it seemed simple, a grey and damp place, almost Earth-like, but the farther I went, the stranger the look of the walls became. They changed to a dark color, but at times, it felt like the walls were moving in a wave-like pattern. When I reached a split in the path, there was a dark, stony tablet sitting against the wall.

I drew closer to it and noticed the changing patterns inside its darkness. I found myself mesmerized and reached out to touch it. My finger made contact, and suddenly, everything around me changed. I was standing in the middle of a street on a black asphalt surface. I looked to my left and saw a familiar building. A small grocery store. Right next to it, a young boy was walking home from school. He was wearing a blue jacket and seemed lost in his thoughts. Wait…. that's me! I'm that boy!

I walked over to him, but the boy simply walked by. He could neither see nor hear me. I followed patiently, and then I remembered. Frantically, I looked to my right. From behind a hedge bounded a large dog with a long face and black and white fur. Its eyes were bloodshot and the mouth with sharp teeth was wide open with foam dripping from it. A crazy rabid dog.

Its tongue hung out, and it went straight for the boy. I kept yelling, and perhaps somehow he did hear me because he saw the dog and began to run.

I followed them. My heart was beating fast. I remembered the terror and the fear.

The boy ran towards a tall, grey apartment building. The dog followed. At the bottom of the building were deep drainage-like square open cellars. The boy jumped into one of these. With fear, he watched the dog stop at the edge, looking down at him with foamy saliva dripping from its mouth. Perhaps seeing that its prey was beyond reach, it snarled and left. I felt relief for myself.

Then, I saw a dark, thin figure in the shrubs across the road. It had dark red eyes, and it pointed at me.

The voice surrounded me again, inside my head, but almost as if it were speaking aloud. "You can rid yourself of all the deep fears of your life. All the trauma. No more pain will enter your life…."

Then, I was back in the cave. One

of the passages was blocked now, and only the left one remained. Not having a choice, I pointed my flashlight and continued despite the chills running down my spine. I hoped not to see that thing again, but I doubted that my wish would come true as I stared into a dark glass on the wall and was sucked into another vision.

It was that same boy…me. I was running around inside a market, surrounded by people. Some sold fresh strawberries, some others farm cheese. There were stands with fake imported clothes. Yet the boy was just running. The boy was scared. I ran after myself, and as I saw a bald man charging for the boy, I began to remember. More fear… more terror.

I watched the boy stumble and stop

as the bald man grabbed him. The boy could see a police car outside, but the bald man showed him the knife under his black jacket and pulled the boy away. "You suck at running, but you still made me run, and you'll pay for that," he said, menacingly.

The boy wasn't a bad runner, but the shock of the situation and the confusion had taken away his strength. I followed them into a dark building where other gang members joined them. They threw the boy up against a wall, and the man took out his knife, holding it close to the boy's face. He could smell the man's sour breath.

"So, what to do with you?"

The vision began to spin, and the words echoed…

What to do

What to do

What to do

The dark figure with red eyes appeared in front of me, and I shook. "You are feeling the fear now, as you had it then. Go to the diamond. Give your life to it, and never feel fear again."

I was once again back in the cave. There was a doorway of sorts, opening into a vast room. It was illuminated thanks to holes in the ceiling, so I turned off my flashlight. I instantly felt the great magnetism inside this room and my eyes were drawn towards the thing in the center.

A large diamond seemed to float in the air. It appeared to be inky black, but as I started to draw closer I could see movement inside of it. There was even black liquid dripping from it onto the floor. I stopped a few meters away, fascinated by the immense power coming from it. Almost a crushing feeling.

My eyes teared up from the pressure in my head as I heard the soft voice speaking directly into my psyche. "Kjell, the majestic master, one who traveled through worlds…your gift awaits you here, as you deserve the best. For far too long, you have been overlooked. Under-appreciated, with your fears driving you away from the things you love. Today it all ends as you receive my gift. No more fear, only power…reach out…and touch me."

I slowly reached out my hand and touched the large floating diamond with the tip of my finger. Some of the black, gooey slime oozed into my hand as I drew it away. Then I saw it all seep into my glove and become absorbed into my skin. I couldn't see my hand, but I could feel the liquid going inside.

My legs wobbled as I felt sick and lightheaded. I dropped onto my knees, and everything began to spin. The ground in front of my eyes disappeared, and another vision began.

A giant black hole was right in front of me, and I floated towards it. From its darkness came a chorus of horrific screams and pleas. They filled the atmosphere around me. I felt sweat dripping into my eyes and I almost took off my helmet, but then I was returned to reality. Everything seemed stable again as I got back up to my feet and looked at the floating diamond.

What was this thing? I decided to leave my questions for later as I could run again, and that's exactly what I did. Funnily enough, I found my way out perfectly, as if something had guided me. I felt like a different person, but I didn't know how different yet.

How different? In what way?

I wish I could say that once I got out of the cave I could breathe in fresh air and relax, but this was Mars, a place of relentless stress and pressure.

I got into the rover and drove back to the lift. As I parked, I noticed that Tugworth had already loaded the panels. "All fixed, I assume," I said, exiting my rover.

Tugworth actually bowed slightly. "That's right, the lift is operational again. We may go up and place the panels. Did you locate the cave?"

"Yes, it was easy to find."

"Was there anything inside?"

I watched him for a moment silently. Why should I tell this robot anything? "No, nothing worth noting."

"Your pulse, heartbeat, and pressure are irregular. Are you sure nothing happened?"

"Let's get the panels, Tugworth, no more questions. Don't waste our daylight."

The robot obeyed, and we got on the lift. It was a powerful device, and once activated, it took us smoothly a good 200 feet up onto a platform where the previous team had everything set up, but the old panels were no longer functioning. We had to detach all of the old panels first and throw them down. It took quite a while. Surprisingly, I felt very strong.

Then, the tedious task of placing the new ones began. From time to time, I felt my right hand twitch in a very violent manner, where the black stuff had been absorbed. Tugworth noticed and surely saved it in his memory to show Astrid.

How I hated this robot! I imagined bashing his metal head in! A smile crept over my face…Then, to my surprise, I thought of Astrid naked on my bed, naked and afraid of me! I shook my head. What the hell was going on?

I saw Tugworth looking at me. "We are almost done, and you are tired. Wait for me at the lift. I'll do the last one myself."

I did not reply to him and simply went over to the lift.

The sun was setting, and watching it, I considered what was happening to my mind and body.

Tugworth hurried back, and with haste, we lowered the lift, quickly getting back into the rovers. As I followed Tugworth, there was very little sunlight left. Then, I noticed a small separate dome.

"There." It was the same voice as in the cave. I slowed my rover and turned to face it.

"What is going on, Kjell?" It was Tugworth on the earpiece.

"No problem, you go on. I need to check something quickly."

"What do I tell Astrid?"

"Part of my job. I have to check out that dome and make sure there is nothing there that we need."

Tugworth went on his way, surely unconvinced. I drove my rover closer to the dome. It was much smaller than any of the other ones, and it was grey all over. I refilled my suit's air supply and went out again.

It was easy to move fast, but I felt the terrible cold coming on as the last sunlight faded away. I turned on my flashlight and went up to the door. There was a code panel. Now what?

"Touch the door." The voice again.

Instinctively, I put my right hand on the door. Dark lines appeared all over my glove like veins coming from my hand, and then the door slid open. I entered and checked the air compression room. It was not functioning. Neither was the light panel. I moved into the darkness of the main room.

Complete silence surrounded me, and in that dark room, I felt a presence.

I unconsciously slowly turned my head, and my flashlight illuminated a tall, thin, dark figure. I simply froze in place as our eyes met.

Its eyes were dark red. The creature raised its hand and pointed towards the other side of the room. Another small door. After glancing at it, I looked back, but the creature was gone. There was no one there anymore. I felt my legs slightly shaking as I walked over to the small door and opened it. Inside a simple oval room lay a pile of various weapons. Laser guns, prolonged battle hammers, electric heavy batons, and guns. I had a few of my own, including one on my hip, but I picked up the electric baton. I felt it was a good addition and a quiet one compared to others.

Why would I think that specifically?

Yet that's the thought that swirled around my head. I had the feeling of being sneaky, secretive, doing something behind others' backs.

I looked around the main room again. No one. Was I hallucinating? I had read many stories of people going insane in space. Could it be that I was one of them?

CHAPTER EIGHT
PART THREE

Darkness had come, and the mad cold seized the Martian land once again, as it did each and every night. Astrid stood by the entrance as Kjell arrived, looking utterly exhausted. The first thing she noticed as he stripped off his gloves were some dark spots on his right hand. "What happened to you? What happened to your hand?!"

Kjell raised his hand to his eye level and stared at it for a moment. Shocked, Astrid realized that he had not noticed the dark spots before she did.

"I have no idea, Astrid. However, I'm tired, and I'll lie down now."

She frowned. "You must report and follow protocol."

"No!" Kjell yelled forcefully, and it shook Astrid. She was speechless. In a more subdued voice, he stated, "I said I'm tired. Good night." Kjell walked to his room, and the door slid shut behind him.

Tugworth came up to Astrid. "I believe that Kjell is having a difficult time."

"You don't say, Tugworth. It looks like a nervous breakdown." She puffed out a breath of air. "We will need medicine for him ready tomorrow. I hope he gets some proper rest and gets his head straight in the morning. I'm going to check a few plants that we transferred and then sleep."

However, it wasn't so easy for

Astrid as she thought back on one of the reports about Dark Aurora. The black spots on the hand…Instead of the botanical garden, Astrid went to her computer and began to look over the Dark Aurora archives.

Astrid patiently scrolled from one document to another on the tablet. More than an hour passed by, and then she finally found the first entry mentioning it. It was written by her mentor, doctor Liardes.

"Today, Harvik and two robots entered the depth of the cave for the first time since the initial scans, measurements, and the first corridor. I tried to contact Harvik several times when we all noticed that the night was fast approaching and he had been inside far too long. However, there was no reply. As we began to assemble a team, we saw a rover coming back, but just one. Only Harvik came back, and the two robots were missing.

"Upon questioning him, Harvik replied rudely and out of character. We did get him to tell us that the robots just collapsed once they went deep inside the cave. An unlikely scenario. I noticed black spots on Harvik's right arm and brought this to his attention; however, he scoffed at me. This is indeed a troubling development."

Astrid stopped reading and leaned back, drinking some water. She had trouble thinking clearly as fear began to take over her mind and body. If something was happening to Kjell, what could she do about it? Perhaps isolation? Quarantine? He'd never say yes, especially in his current state, and there was just one quarantine room, so it wouldn't be easy to trick him.

Astrid knew what could help her to clear her mind. Late or not, she went to the garden. Nothing made her feel better than seeing those plants strive despite their incredible location and circumstances.

If plants could find a way to survive in the most dire circumstances, so could she.

Astrid turned in the dimmed night light and stepped over to a plant with long, dark red leaves. As she sat down and stroked one of them, she suddenly felt the unpleasant sensation of being watched. She quickly turned around and saw a dark figure move among the tall plants. Astrid jumped up to her feet, feeling her heart rate elevate instantly.

She frantically searched with her eyes for any weapon but was out of luck.

"Bella? Tugworth? Please come here!"

Nothing. Then she saw it.

In the farthest and darkest corner of the dome stood a tall, slim, dark figure. Its dark red eyes met hers, and Astrid screamed.

She woke up in a cold sweat, still at her reading table. "Dear God!" She realized she had never left the room to see the garden, and after that vision, she wasn't about to. She lay down in bed and pulled her blanket over her face, shivering with fear.

In the morning, things did not ease. As the Mars sunbeams illuminated the rooms, Kjell was the first one up. He sat in the corner, away from Astrid, gulping down coffee after coffee, not eating any food.

Astrid requested that Bella and Tugworth be by her side as she approached Kjell. "Good morning, Kjell. How did you sleep? Are you feeling better?"

"Look, it's the band of weird misfits. Robots created by incompetent people and a nerd with no social skills." Kjell gulped more coffee.

Irritated, Astrid replied, "This is very immature, Kjell; you cannot control yourself. We will have to put you into quarantine."

"You and what army? Bitch…"

Astrid stood frozen and stunned at his disrespect but was even more shocked that he stood up with his hand on his gun, which was thankfully still in the holster.

"What? Can't speak anymore? I'm going out. We got important work to do, and you're babbling here."

As Kjell stormed off, Astrid shook her head and instructed Tugworth to follow him. Then she sent Bella away to check on the garden and sank into a chair, folding her arms and putting her head down on the table.

How had it come to this? Why? This mission was so important! It was her dream. Now, she was stuck with someone whom she believed had gone insane, and she had not yet heard about the exact date of arrival of the second ship. She had not told Kjell that she had received a transmission indicating that the the second ship was on its way to Mars again.

Astrid got up and grabbed her tablet, and began to write down everything that had been happening. She planned to send reports so that everyone on the second ship knew the details.

Meanwhile, Kjell took the rover straight to the cave. Tugworth parked his at a distance, and did not go in. Hours passed before Kjell emerged again. As they drove back, obviously, Kjell could see the other rover and he was not one bit pleased. "Damn robot...soon you'll pay."

"The woman also," said the voice inside Kjell's head.

He remained silent. Kjell was still fighting and resisting the spread of the dark corruption, but it was taking more and more from him.

Many days went by and Astrid

worked to keep her distance from Kjell, who spent all of his days in the cave, which meant that she and Bella had to take on all the responsibilities and duties on the ship.

One of the nights when Kjell returned, Astrid noticed black spots appearing on his neck. "Tugworth," she said to the robot after Kjell went to his room, "you will need to enter the cave and see what Kjell is doing in there." Of course, the robot would follow her instructions.

Kjell got up the next morning as usual. He guzzled down mugs of coffee and did not eat. He hadn't eaten in days, and his body had become gaunt, his cheeks sunken, and his neck, the skin loose and covered with black spots, began to look like that of a goose. Kjell's eyes were weary and now had a tint of red-brown color rather than his natural light green.

Looking like the cosmic ghoul, Kjell got into the rover and continued with his new routine. However, this time, Tugworth parked his rover right next to the cave after he watched Kjell enter. The robot was well-programmed and took all precautions to keep itself from danger. According to its calculations, the probability of something dangerous happening was high.

The robot's AI learned from experience, and Tugworth was a robot with vast experience. He was a new model, but his programmed memory system was the same computer brain from a previous robot, just upgraded with the latest technology. In fact, Tugworth had been around for 70 years. Constantly upgraded, he was one of a kind. This was the primary reason he had been the first choice robot for this particular mission. It also meant that his calculations were rarely wrong.

One advantage Tugworth had was that he could see in the dark, and it meant he would not be exposed by turning on a flashlight. Silently, Tugworth walked along the wall of the cave, turning up his hearing capabilities to the maximum. Yet, so far, he could only catch distant magnetic sounds of unknown origin. He found it confusing to his system that he was unable to perform his thermal life scans. Something was jamming them. Perhaps the magnetism he could hear.

Of course, Tugworth did not feel fear or worry, but within him was installed a self-preservation program, so he was more careful than even many humans could be.

When he reached a split in the tunnel of the cave, he chose the corridor from which the sounds were coming. There was still no sign of Kjell.

As Tugworth neared the source, he began to glitch in various ways. His systems were going haywire. In spite of this, he finally emerged into the vast big room with the large black floating diamond in its center. Moving in a rather limited way due to the issues he was experiencing, Tugworth tried to scan the diamond but failed. The very next moment, Kjell was behind the robot and smashed him on the head with a rock. Tugworth fell to the ground, not far from the black diamond.

"I…I…my calculations…"

Kjell stood above him, smiling with a gun pointing right at his head. "Goodnight, tin man."

CHAPTER NINE
NOT THERE

So many full moons ago…so many years ago…Time…we think we can measure it but in truth we cannot even begin to comprehend it.

Jack sat by the window of the spaceship looking at a photo of his team. All of them were dead, except for him. It seemed just yesterday when they all sat together at the bar and talked about car racing.

Besides this, the fact that he still had to go to Mars really made him uneasy. Yes, he was considered the "unbreakable soldier," but now that title seemed to have reached its limit. *Even the strongest foundation will eventually crumble*, he thought, *because no one can defeat time*.

Jack looked at the blue liquid in his glass. A mix of minerals and vitamins for a faster recovery. So he could perform his duties on Mars upon arrival.

"How are you feeling today?" It was the familiar voice of the man who had saved him.

Tom stood behind him. Jack slowly turned his head. "Why do you even ask anymore, Tom?"

"Because it's important."

"It'll be the same answer every time. Even when the bruises and injuries are all good. It'll still be the same answer. I'm done with all this, yet I have to still provide the proper quality of work upon arrival."

Tom placed a hand on Jack's

shoulder. "You are a top professional. You were chosen as a leader based on your mental strength, besides other qualifications," he said, comfortingly.

"Heh…Yeah, Tom…Because we totally expected to run into a ship full of demons!"

Tom stepped back a bit, seeing rage appear in Jack's eyes. "I'm sorry, but don't forget how many of my men, friends, died as well.

"You know," he went on, "I was preparing for the early stages of a project called Tricunius when I got the call. I had no idea what horror could have been lying ahead. I thought it was going to be a clear-cut mission. Kill some creatures, go home."

This comment seemed to calm Jack down as he shook his head. "I'm sorry,

Tom. Are you reading the manuals? With the state I'm in, you might have to help out once we are there."

"I am. I'll do my best. Rest up." Tom walked away, and Jack was alone again. He looked at his main bite wound. Even after all the medicine and injections, it still looked inflamed. What other things were there to worry about? There were a total of nine men on this ship now, and Juniper the robot. A bigger crew than first expected for Mars, which meant more trouble. There wasn't a single positive thing Jack could force into his head as he chugged the blue liquid and grimaced. Not the best tasting stuff.

Across the ship several other men were also recovering from injuries, while still others were studying and preparing for Mars. Tom sat by Juniper, who was now manually flying the ship, since the automatic system had been damaged from the detachment and explosion of Dark Aurora.

"Juniper, how many supplies do we have on this ship? How long will they last for all of the men?"

"If the men eat two meals a day instead of three, then we should make it until the shipment comes in. We will also be growing gardens in the domes. Vegetables, fruits, nuts."

"Ah, well, that's good to hear. You give me more hope."

"Is that how you get hope?"

Jack gave a wry smile. "Well, sometimes we have to find any positive even in the worst situations and use those. Otherwise, things will seem even worse."

"Very interesting."

"For you, it's all about computing and putting the percentages together, isn't it?"

"Of course. The probabilities, but I am aware of the things that humans call miracles and willpower. While I can't understand these, being aware of them helps me to always leave some room for something outside the calculations."

"Fascinating. Well, Juniper, I'm glad you don't sleep, but I, on the other hand, been up for 18 hours, so I'll see you in six hours."

Jack went to his bunk and fell asleep, but his dreams were more like deadly visions.

Jack stood outside of a cave. He was clearly on Mars, judging by all of the red sand around him and the spacesuit he wore. Suddenly, dull cries began to come from a black cave, and one by one, his dead friends emerged from the darkness. They had black collars around their necks, and right behind them was a tall, slim, black creature with dark red eyes, holding them all on leashes. Jack wanted to do something but felt unable to move. His body was not his own. His feet and legs began to move towards the cave. Jack screamed and begged, but he was taken into the darkness. Once inside, he was forced to his knees, bowing down to a black diamond that seemed to float in midair. He sensed that it was the source of the power that held him.

Jack sat up in bed with a cold sweat on his face. His wound was throbbing. The vision was still clear in his mind. He knew it was real. However, what troubled him more was that the walls of his room were slightly moving from side to side. It was either the medications affecting him or a fever from the infection.

"No way I'm going there…not there…That's the source of it all!" Jack pressed the buttons on the wall panel, and a few seconds later, he heard Tom's voice through the speaker.

"What's wrong, Jack?"

"Tom, turn this ship around. The source of those creatures is at that base on Mars. Tell the other crew to leave, too!"

There was a pause, and then Tom's voice changed to one of deep concern. "Jack, I'll have the guys bring you some more meds. Please, I know this is tough, but try not to alarm the rest of the crew. We are almost there, you know this. The landing procedures will begin soon.

Please just strap up inside your room and wait."

The transmission was cut by Jack as he stood up clutching his fists and grinding his teeth. "Alarm them, alarm them…" Jack grabbed his gun and made sure it was fully loaded. "Not there…not there…not going there…"

Jack's mind was becoming frantic. The infection had finally affected his neurons, and the void within the black diamond had access to him. Jack was in the worst place in both worlds. The darkness that was influencing him and his own fear and depression. Only one thought obsessed him: "Not there."

Jack peeked out the door of his room, and he saw the two men coming with his medications. He ran across the corridor and turned into another one. It was a straight run to the control center where Juniper was piloting the ship.

He could hear the two men running behind him and sending voice messages to Tom. A moment later the alert began to buzz through every part of the ship.

Jack made it into the command center before they could cut him off and shut the sliding metal door. Juniper turned around, confused. "What is going on, Jack? All of your scans are too high."

"Shut up already!" Jack screeched and blasted the robot with one straight shot through the head. Then he began smashing the controls.

Tom and the other crew members finally forced the door open and were met with deadly fire, dropping two crew members instantly. Jack hid behind a large control panel and kept firing. There was no point in trying to reason with him now.

Tom provided cover for two other men as they attempted to circle, but they were no match for Jack, as he gunned them down ruthlessly. He was a top combat expert, possessed by the darkness. Tom was alone now, as the only other two crewmen were in the medical bay, still too injured to do much.

Jack got a perfect shot when Tom exposed his gun. Tom's right hand was blasted off, and now Jack stood over him, looking demented.

"No! Jack! Snap out of it!"

Jack killed Tom with a shot through the head and continued destroying the control room.

The spaceship was going down.

CHAPTER TEN
THE DARKNESS COMES

It was the fire coming from the sky...
or rather the fiery spaceship crashing
down violently during the cold Mars
night. Standing on top of a short rocky
formation in his space suit, Kjell wore a
crazed, maniacal grimace. His eyes had
begun turning a dark red, and his skin
was mottled with black all over his body.
The smile he had dancing upon his face
was one of nightmares. He rejoiced in the
spaceship crash. Despite the abnormal
cold, he ran to his rover and began to
drive towards the crash site.

Meanwhile, at the domes, Astrid
stood by the window in the garden, and

her expression was one of absolute horror. The moment she had lost contact with the others, she'd suspected something, but this was the worst-case scenario. And Kjell…He had cut all transmissions with her, and Tugworth had never returned. She feared for the worst.

Astrid turned to the remaining robot, Bella. "Bella, get our spaceship ready for a split-away rocket launch."

"But why? Aren't we staying for the mission?"

"I think we must be ready. This mission has been compromised, Bella. Please set all of the controls on autopilot to Earth and prepare everything for launch. Load up enough tubes as well."

"How about the garden?"

"We will take the seeds and plant them in the small pots. We will still have one small room for them on the flight back."

"What do you want me to do after setup?"

"Be back here with a weapon, and don't let Kjell get near the ship."

"But I'm not programmed for combat."

Astrid squared her shoulders. "Just hold the weapon and talk to him, stall for time."

They began the work. It was devastating for Astrid, but she knew they had to move fast, and she could dwell on the sadness later.

Meanwhile, the rover rushed through the dunes. Kjell could see everything in the dark, thanks to his new eyes. He just couldn't stop laughing. What a demented joy it was to give himself to the black diamond and its voice that now lived inside his head. The utter darkness was in full control.

Kjell parked the rover right outside the crash site and, upon getting out, immediately noticed the wobbling silhouette of a man in a space suit slowly emerging from the fire. He ran towards it.

The man in the suit was Jack, and he reached his hand towards Kjell. "Help…"

Kjell kicked him, knocking him down upon the sand, and then tied his hands behind his back with a thin cable he had brought with him, anticipating the possibility of a survivor.

"What…are you doing?" Jack had a hard time talking.

Kjell's voice had now transformed

and had a hissing quality with a low vibration. "You did not want to see usss….but you cannot escape it…the master will greet you now…in person…"

"No…No! Stop…not there…" Jack screamed, fighting the handcuff.

Kjell giggled maniacally. "You are coming with me, and your blood shall be given to my masssster."

He dragged Jack across the sand and loaded him up into the rover. Jack had no strength to fight. He could only faintly plead for mercy, but none was going to come.

"You'll meet your maker sssoon, Jack! Oh boy, Jack, you have no idea how wonderful it is…to be chosssen! You could have been too, but you denied the giftssss...such a shame."

Once at the cave entrance, Kjell

dropped a narrow chain around Jack's neck and fastened the other end around his own body. He violently dragged Jack through the stony corridors and out into the large room where the black diamond was floating in the air.

The cave was full of whispers, and many thin, dark creatures appeared out of the shadows. They chanted in a low voice as a black dagger emerged from the black diamond and fell into Kjell's hand. He pulled Jack into a spot beneath the black diamond.

Jack got one last scream out before Kjell pierced his heart with the dagger. The sacrifice was complete. Jack's blood floated into the air and into the black diamond, then it came out as black blood and flowed towards Kjell, who took off his helmet, allowing the black blood to enter his body as he stood there, convulsing.

The essence of darkness was now fully within him, and he knew that his final true mission was to bring this gift to Earth. With eyes fully red, Kjell ran back to his rover. "I'm coming, Astrid!" he singsonged.

Bella had prepared everything at this point and stood in front of the ship's doors, awkwardly holding a rifle. She looked very much out of her element. Astrid felt badly about leaving her there. She still hoped that they would both make it out of this horrific situation, but she was more determined that she and not Kjell would survive the mission. The possession that had affected Kjell could be contagious, and Astrid figured that was probably why it had wanted to take

Dark Aurora in the first place: to corrupt other worlds.

Astrid was in the first dome, just outside the spaceship, which was getting ready to depart, when she saw Kjell's rover. He parked outside of the main dome as she suspected he might. Then, what she saw truly shook her. Kjell jumped out of the rover without a helmet! And he was fine!

Kjell opened the main doors and stopped in his tracks as Bella stood in front of him. "Look at that…sacrificing a friend. I knew Astrid had it in her, too. She will love my master. Together, we will bring it to Earth and make them all believers!"

"Sir, Kjell, please do not enter…"

"Hahahah!!! Ohhh! Ohhhhh! So good!" Kjell whipped out his pistol and put a hole in Bella's face. The robot collapsed, emitting sparks as she hit the floor.

"Such awful things…" Kjell tsked. He went inside the dome smiling, but his face changed into one of anger as he saw that all the domes, including the garden, had been set on fire. He ran towards the door of the garden and got in, but the flames were engulfing everything, and his skin was starting to burn as he tried to force his way through. "The crazy bitch torched everything!" he screamed. Then he suddenly began to laugh uncontrollably, spreading his arms and spinning in the flames.

The rocket with the space shuttle had been launched. In the final moment, Astrid saw Kjell in the flames through the dome's window. He was smiling.

Was it just her imagination? The trauma of the terror?

Astrid took in a deep breath, strapped up tightly. She had a long trip ahead of her.

As she left Mars and the failed mission, Astrid remembered, despite the horror, her wish, and the dream.

Sometimes we will have more pain from a dream coming true rather than not. It turned out that the best life was one focused on the present, taking care of each day, a step at a time. Living in a distant dream, waiting to be happy when it was fulfilled, was a life that had robbed her of the true human experience of the journey.

One day, her shock and horror were going to ease. She had learned the hard lesson and would live…

One day at a time.

The End

Alexander Semenyuk (also known as Oleksandr Semenyuk) is a Ukrainian-American author. He was born in Lutsk, Ukraine, in 1986. At 14, he immigrated to the United States. Alexander's favorite genres are sci-fi, horror, and fantasy. Early in life, Alexander was greatly influenced by classic literature and, since childhood, dreamed of becoming a writer.